D1630859

Celebrating 30 years of a children's classic

Through My Window was inspired by people Eileen knew and events observed from her own windows in 1980s London. She worked with young children from many ethnic backgrounds who rarely saw themselves in books. "Put us in your books!" they said. Tony developed the story and the rest is history. In the U.S. and the U.K., *Through My Window* was the first picture book published with a mixed race family, where the story wasn't about race or culture. The book has remained in print for 30 years, and now it has been reissued for a new generation of children to enjoy.

For Islington Library Staff

Based on an original idea by Eileen Browne

First published in Great Britain in 1986 by
Methuen Children's Books Ltd

This edition first published in the UK in 2016
by Frances Lincoln Children's Books,
74-77 White Lion Street, London N1 9PF
www.franceslincoln.com

A CIP catalogue record for this book is available from the British Library.

ISBN 978-1-84780-756-4

Printed in China

1 3 5 7 9 8 6 4 2

THROUGH MY WINDOW

Tony Bradman &
Eileen Browne

Frances Lincoln
Children's Books

Jo was ill in the night.
In the morning she had a temperature
and her dad said
she would have to stay indoors.

She wanted her mum
to stay at home, too.
But she had to go to work.

"Never mind, Jo.
Keep an eye out for me tonight –
I'll bring you a surprise
to make you feel better."

So Jo waved goodbye
to her mum
from the window
until she turned the corner
of the street.

Jo felt tired,
so she had a sleep.

When she woke up,
she heard feet
coming up the street.

Was it her mum
coming home
with her surprise?
She looked out
of the window.

But it was only Jo's friend,
the postman.
He waved, but he didn't have
any letters for Jo's flat today.

Jo looked at some books.
After a while she heard feet
coming up the street again
and a clinking,
clanking sound.
Was it her mum
coming home
with her surprise?

She looked out of the window.
But it was only her friend,
the milkman.
"Hello, Jo," he called,
and left some milk
outside their door.

Jo's dad brought her lunch
on a tray.

When she'd finished,
she heard some more feet
coming up the street.

Was it her mum coming home
with her surprise?
She looked out of the window.

But it was only her friend,
Mrs Ali, who lived next door.
"I've brought you some comics,"
said Mrs Ali,
and came in to see her.

Jo looked at the comics
and then she heard some barking
in the street.
Was it Jo's mum coming home
with a surprise that barked?

She looked out of the window.
But it was only Patch,
Mrs Ali's dog,
chasing a cat across the road.

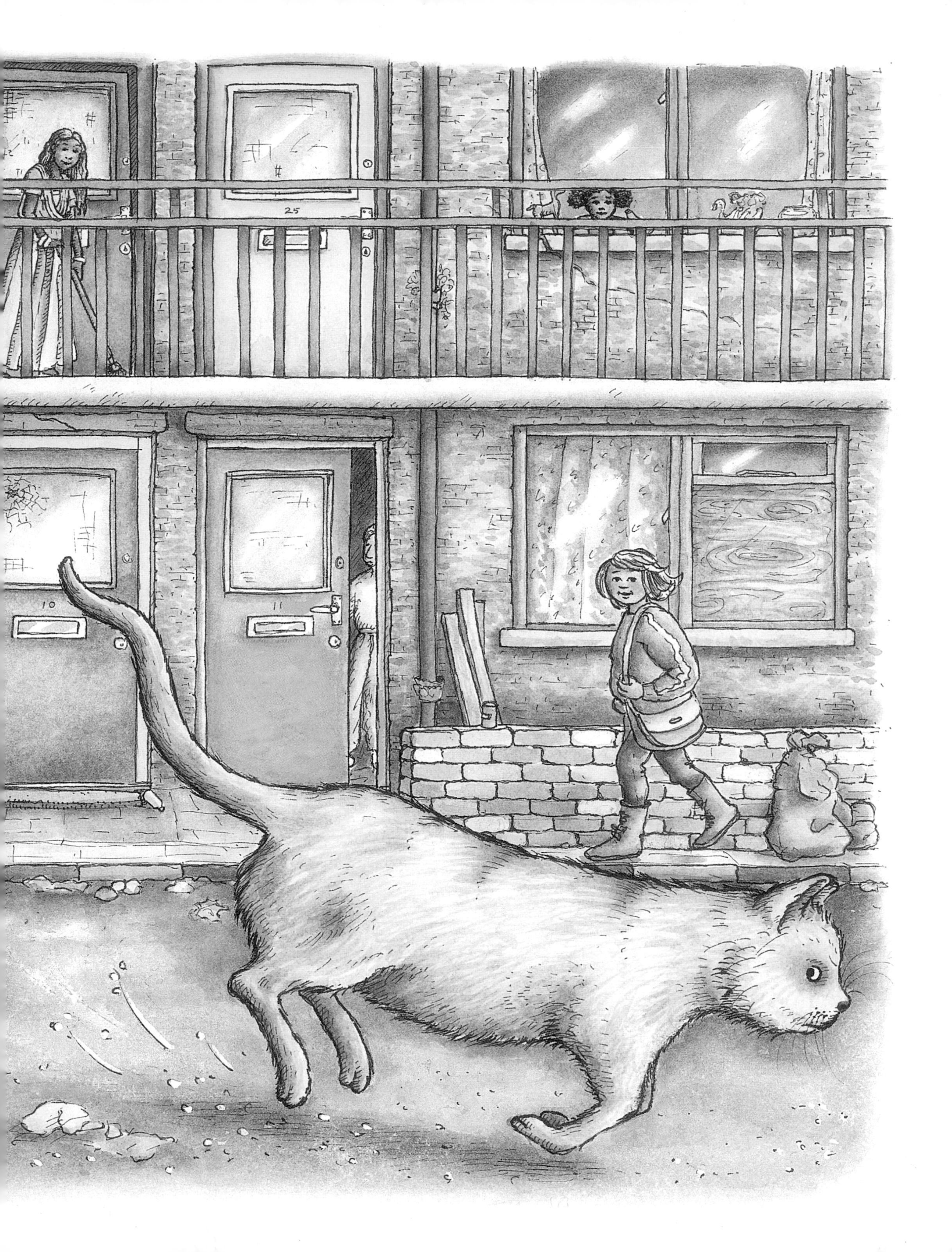
25
10
11

Jo felt tired so
she had another sleep.
She dreamed about all the things
her mum might bring her
as a surprise.

Then she dreamed that she could
hear feet in the street again,
and woke up.
Was it her mum coming home
with her surprise?

She looked out of the window.
But it was only her friend
the window cleaner.

The window cleaner
pressed her face
against the glass
and made Jo laugh.

But soon Jo was fed up.
Her mum would be ages yet.
And she'd probably forget
all about her surprise, anyway.

Jo heard some more feet
coming up the street.
They were coming closer,
and closer, and closer.

Was it Jo's mum coming home
with her surprise?
Jo looked out of the window.

Yes it was!
She ran down the hall
and opened the door for her mum.

“Here you are, Jo.
Here’s a present
to make you feel better.”

Jo opened the box.
And can you guess
what was inside it?

That's right –

the present she'd always wanted!

MORE CLASSIC CHILDREN'S TITLES
PUBLISHED BY FRANCES LINCOLN CHILDREN'S BOOKS

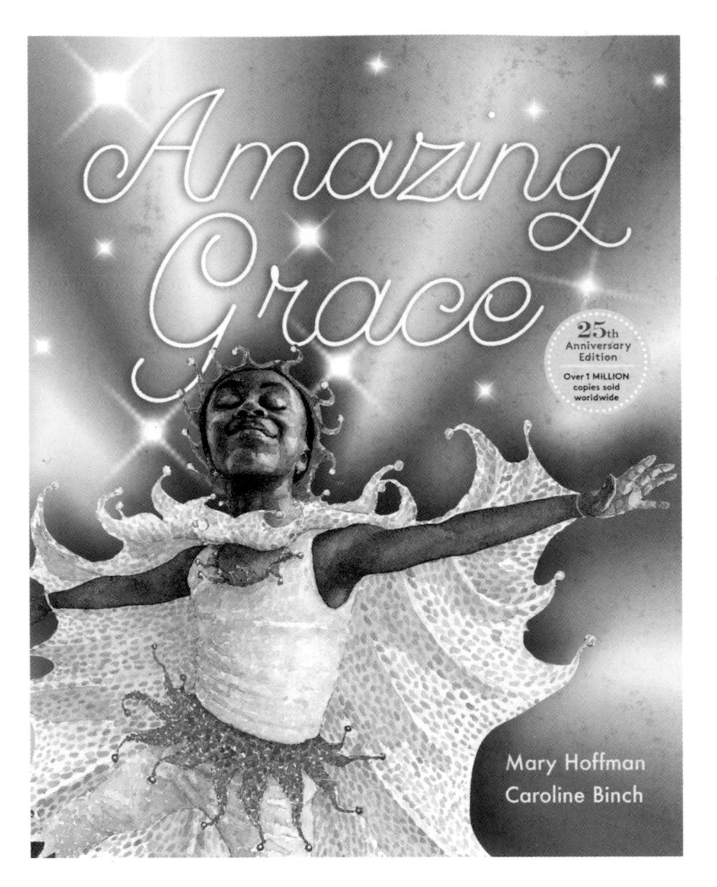

Amazing Grace
978-1-84780-593-5

Written by Mary Hoffman
Illustrated by Caroline Binch

Grace loves to act out stories. Sometimes she plays the leading part, sometimes she is 'a cast of thousands.' When her school decides to perform Peter Pan, Grace is longing to play Peter, but her classmates say that Peter was a boy, and besides, he wasn't black... But Grace's Ma and Nana tell her she can be anything she wants if she puts her mind to it.

"One of those simple yet profoundly moving stories that confronts sexism and racism, accepts they exist, and transcends them through a child's honesty, humour, imagination and hope." — *The Times*

Booktrust 100 Best Books for children in the last 100 years

Seven Stories Diverse Voices – one of the top 50 titles celebrating cultural diversity